*In memory
of summer days with Walter*

An Addisonian Press Book

KIYA
THE
GULL

written and illustrated
by Fen H. Lasell

Addison-Wesley

The Addison-Wesley Publishing Company, Inc., Reading, Massachusetts
Library of Congress catalog card number 77–88688
Printed in the United States of America
First Printing

Kiya was a free bird. From dawn to dusk he swept the sky, the sand, the sea, with all the other sea gulls, scavenging for food. He kept a close eye on the harbor to pick up after fishermen. On the beach he watched the children and ate the sandwiches they couldn't finish. When he came too close, the children cried, "Look! Look at the sea gull!"

After a storm, Kiya and the other gulls cleaned up the tidal marshes. They were willing to eat almost anything, and were still hungry.

Kiya began the day before the sun was up. He left the little island where he lived and went first to the harbor to be present when the fishermen came in to clean their fish. This morning no fishermen were in, but the tide was out, leaving on the pebbles a bundle of seaweed and marsh hay, tangled in baling wire and promising all kinds of delicious pickings. Kiya circled the bundle and when he found it quite harmless, he fell to work. The more he picked, the more he found. But the wire got in his way. He must untangle the straw and seaweeds before he could reach the mussels and crabs that hid within. He tugged and pushed at the wire until one end came free. Kiya put his head in the opening and pulled out the straw.

His efforts attracted other early gulls looking for breakfast. Gull after gull came down to join him. Amid a gleeful shrieking and flapping of wings, they tore at the seaweed and pulled at the wire. They ate what they could and flew away with snails and mussels in their bills, to break the hard shells by dropping them on the rocks.

When the party was over, Kiya found that now it was he who was tangled in baling wire.

"Kiya-kiya-kiya-kiya. . . ," he cried.

The more he struggled, the tighter the wire pulled. At last he freed his wings, but the metal strap looped over his back and bound one leg so he could not move it.

A boy was sitting in his boat watching the gulls. Now, when he saw Kiya's plight, he walked up the pier and jumped down on the pebbles. Kiya saw him coming; he saw the boy stretch out his hands. Kiya flapped his wings and tore himself away from the ground despite the pain of the wire cutting into his back and leg. The boy ran after him, but Kiya rose out of his reach.

He glided over to the beach, lost his balance trying to land on one foot, and came to rest on the cool hard sand at the water's edge. The dragging wire bounced on the sand behind him.

But people were already gathering on the beach for a summer's day in the sun. "Look at that sea gull!" someone called. "He's all caught up in something." People ran toward him. Hands reached for him. He hopped away on one leg, and, beating his wings, managed to raise himself again.

He flew to the high dune where the sea gulls perch at noon. The other gulls were still away looking for their morning meal. Hungry as Kiya was, it hurt him too much to fly. He wanted only to be left in peace. He settled on the highest mound, which let him see in all directions, and there he rested.

Then children came to climb the dune in order to slide down the warm sand. "Look!" they cried. "That sea gull is all tangled up."

Kiya watched as the children slowly surrounded him. Closer and closer they crept until Kiya spread his wings and tried to fly. The wire tore at his flesh. "Catch him!" cried the children. Kiya was grateful he had landed on the highest spot; from there he was able to rise above the children's hands. They leaped to catch at the wire, but missed.

After this second escape, he settled on the water where the cool waves lapped his cuts. He bobbed on the waves while the currents gently drew him out to sea. How was he going to rid himself of this fetter? How was he going to find something to eat?

And then there was that boy again, bearing down on him in his boat. Kiya tried to swim away, but with only one leg paddling it was hard to keep from going in circles. The boy brought his boat into the wind and drifted toward the tangled bird. Kiya again saw two hands reaching for him. Frantically he beat his wings in an effort to raise himself away from the water and the grasping hands. The boat was at a standstill now and Kiya was able to escape, dangling the wire in the water behind him.

Where could he go but back to his island? There were too many people on the mainland forever trying to catch him. In all his life no one had ever tried to catch him before. Why now, that he was in pain?

He made an awkward landing on his favorite perch. At first the other gulls gave him his place on the roof of the deserted island shack, but when they saw his cuts and

his burden of wire, they eyed him with suspicion. He was not one of them any more. He was tangled and bloody and there was no place on the roof for one like him. A newcomer flying in pushed him and Kiya lost his balance. Then all at once the other sea gulls turned on him and drove him to the ground. Kiya dragged his wire to a respectful distance and hid in the salt grass.

When evening brought home still more gulls, Kiya had
to limp to the other side of the island to avoid their biting
bills and beating wings. There, while trying to reach the
height of the knoll, the baling wire caught in a bayberry
bush and he was held fast. His thrashing only tightened
the bond around him.

The sun was low in the West when the boat appeared,
bringing the boy to the island. The boy dropped anchor
in the cove below the knoll. Kiya saw him wade ashore

carrying a small pack and make his way to the other side of the island where the gulls were settling down for the night. A shrieking clamor and confusion of wings greeted the boy's arrival.

Kiya was well hidden where he was. If he didn't move, the boy would never find him and darkness would protect him soon.

But the boy came back to the cove and built a fire out of gathered driftwood. Kiya watched the orange sparks rise into the night. He was weary from his painful day and sleep comforted him.

During the night he woke to find the fire still glowing on the beach below. Toward morning the embers had gone out but the boy still lay there sleeping in his blanket. Now was the time for Kiya to escape before the boy woke and discovered him.

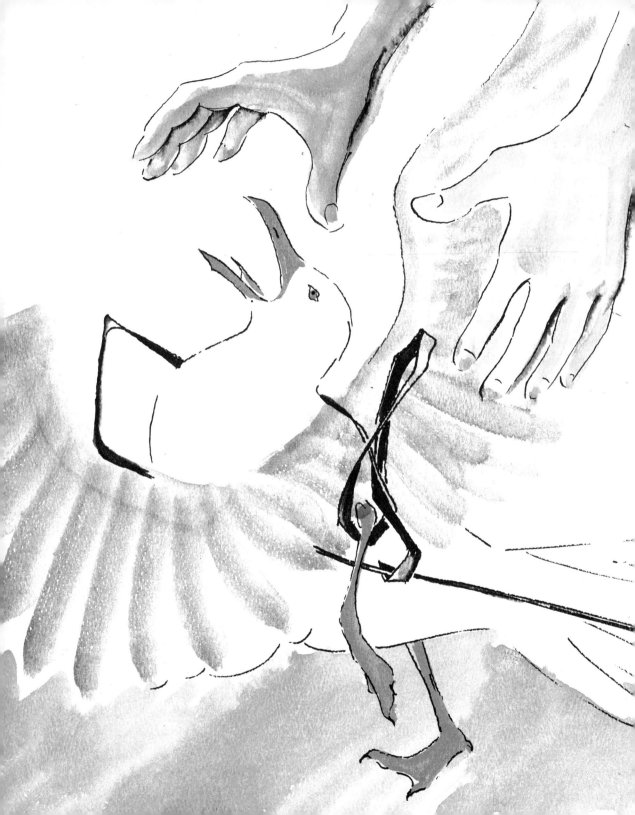

He threw his weight against the wire and fought the unyielding bayberry bush. He beat his raw wings with renewed courage. "Kiya-kiya-kiya-kiya." The commotion woke the boy on the beach. He climbed the knoll and stood above Kiya, looking. They stared at one another, bird and boy, and Kiya knew his time had come. He pecked fiercely at the reaching hand, but the boy closed it over his head.

"Easy now, easy," said the boy, as he struggled with the wire. Kiya gave up trying to fight. The boy unhooked the metal strap and drew it over the gull's head. Then he wound it off the leg. "Easy there." The gull lay still. The hand released his head. Both hands lifted him gently and set him on his feet. Kiya put his weight on his injured leg. He tried to take a step and staggered, but found that he could walk. He blinked and stared at the boy, his pursuer, standing above him. The hands weren't grasping for him any longer. Those hands had freed him of the baling wire.

The boy asked, "Will you be all right?"

Kiya spread his wings and felt that he was free. When he flapped his wings there was no cutting wire. Though he was weak, he could fly. Slowly he rose into the air and circled the boy who was staring up at him. He hovered there a moment tasting the morning breeze, then wheeled and glided down to the water to bob a while on the waves.

Why had he been so frightened of the boy with the reaching hands?

Kiya often flew over the harbor and the beach that summer. There were many boys. There were many boats. Was there one among them who had freed him from the baling wire?

And the boy with the boat looked up and wondered, of all those sea gulls circling above, was there one he knew? Which was the gull he'd saved?